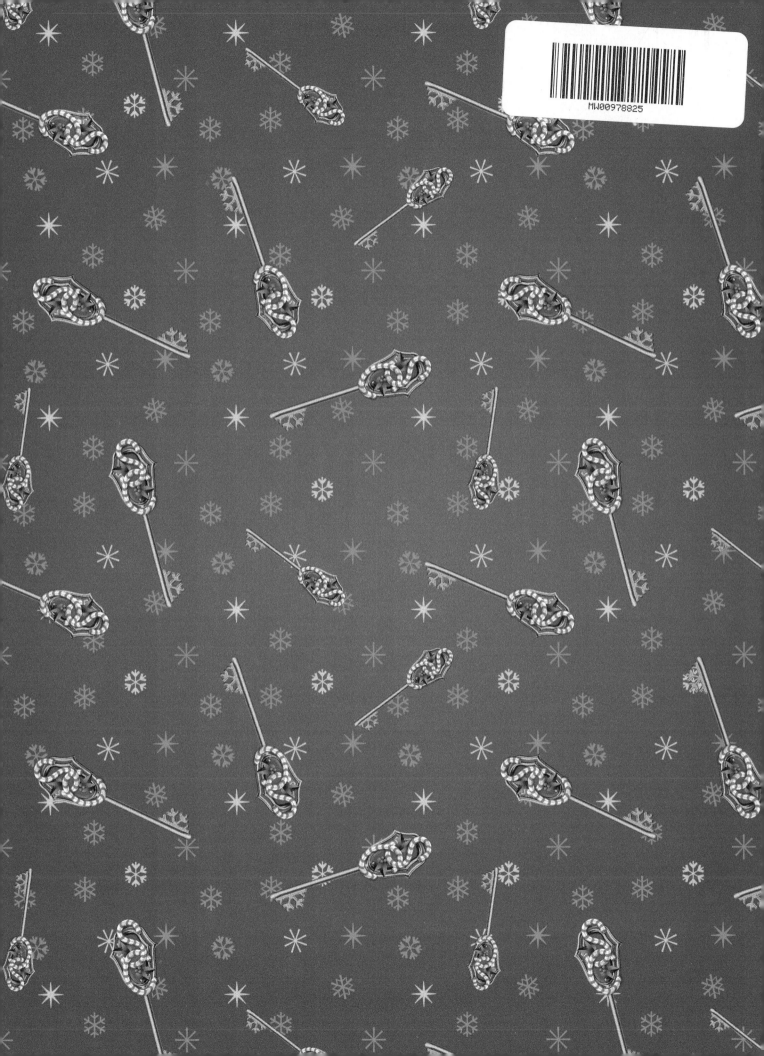

For the Christmas joy that lives
in children's hearts and to my daughters,
Wendy and Robin, who inspired this story.

A special thanks to Michelle Glush
for her Magic Key illustration.

Archway Publishing books may be ordered through booksellers or by contacting:

Archway Publishing
1663 Liberty Drive
Bloomington, IN 47403
www.archwaypublishing.com
1 (888) 242-5904

Because of the dynamic nature of the Internet, any web addresses or links contained in this book may have changed since publication and may no longer be valid. The views expressed in this work are solely those of the author and do not necessarily reflect the views of the publisher, and the publisher hereby disclaims any responsibility for them.

Any people depicted in stock imagery provided by Getty Images are models, and such images are being used for illustrative purposes only.
Certain stock imagery © Getty Images.

This is a work of fiction. All of the characters, names, incidents, organizations, and dialogue in this novel are either the products of the author's imagination or are used fictitiously.

ISBN: 978-1-4808-6699-7 (sc)
ISBN: 978-1-4808-6697-3 (hc)
ISBN: 978-1-4808-6698-0 (e)

Print information available on the last page.

Archway Publishing rev. date: 9/27/2018

Santa's Magical Key

No Chimney? No Problem!

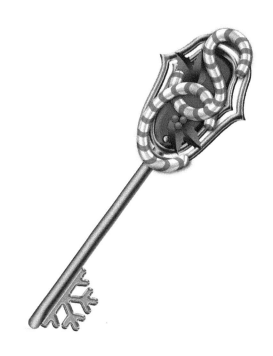

Karen Lucas

'Twas the night before Christmas,
Santa was busy
With gifts to deliver he
almost felt dizzy.

His job's not easy there
are so many toys—
And, flying here and there
to good girls and boys.

Now the stockings are hung —
but the chimney's not there!
Santa has to get *in* to leave
presents — but where?

For years you've been wondering,
wanting to know—
How Santa gets *in*, it's a
mystery, and so . . .

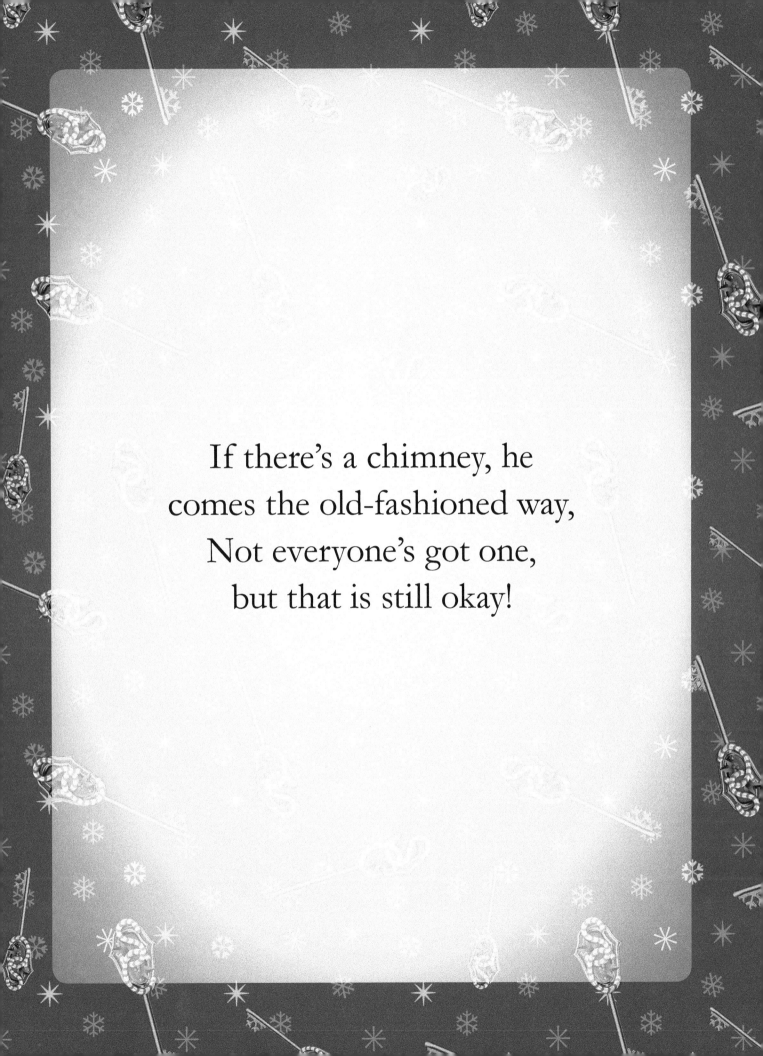

If there's a chimney, he
comes the old-fashioned way,
Not everyone's got one,
but that is still okay!

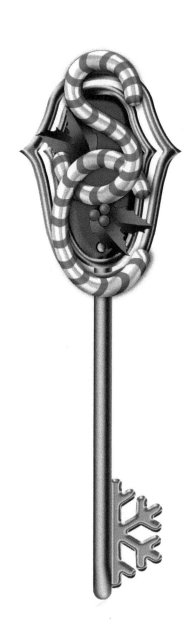

Don't worry or fret about
locked doors and latches,
His magic key works so
your door always matches!

Sometimes the key's tiny,
or grows to be big.
But it always fits your
door's thingamajig.

He doesn't need to deliver
toys from the roof –
There are other ways
and here is the proof.

A fire escape works
for Santa, it seems.
He'll unload the presents,
while you have sweet dreams.

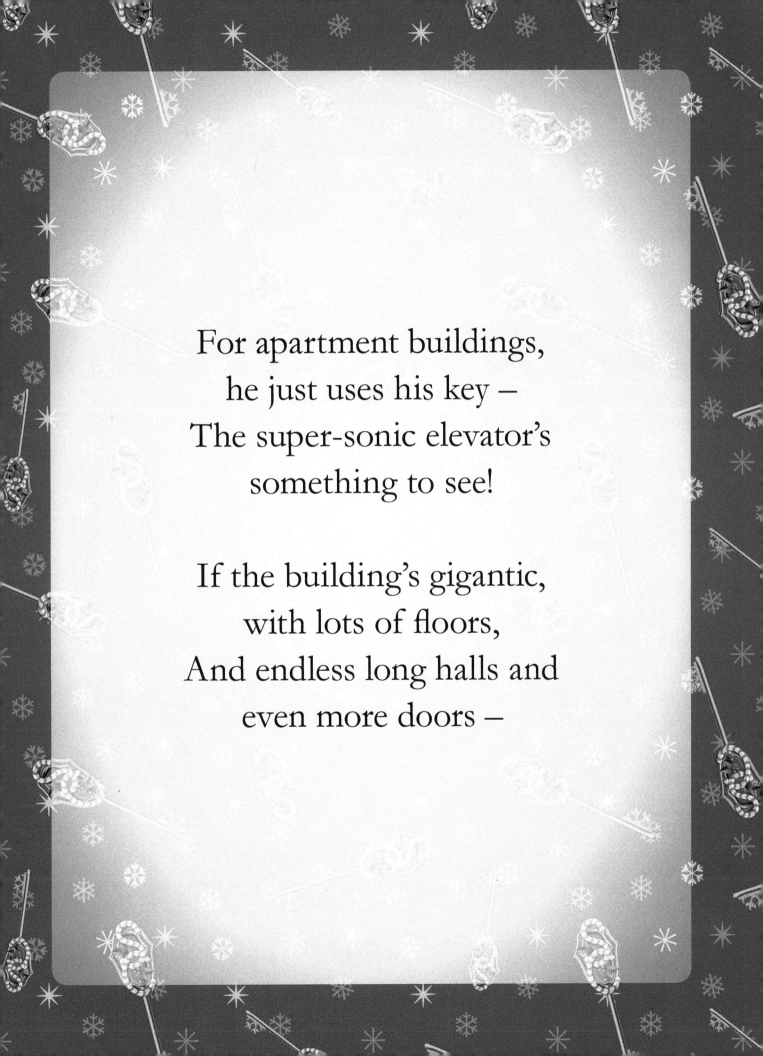

For apartment buildings,
he just uses his key –
The super-sonic elevator's
something to see!

If the building's gigantic,
with lots of floors,
And endless long halls and
even more doors –

Santa has a plan, so you really shouldn't worry. He'll roller skate *in* to bring toys in a hurry!

And whether your house is large or is small –
Santa can find you—no trouble at all!

Even if you visit Aunt Jane in Illinois—
He finds where you're staying
and leaves you a toy.

Don't be too sad if the ball was blue not red,
Or he didn't have room this year on his sled.
Just ask again next year, say please, don't insist.
He'll put a gold X by your name on his list.

Like the Christmas of old,
when that star shined above –
Always remember each gift comes with love.

Merry Christmas

Santa's magic key helps deliver
his toys when due –
So good night, sleep well, and
Merry Christmas to you!

CPSIA information can be obtained
at www.ICGtesting.com
Printed in the USA
BVHW051019151121
621635BV00004B/134